David Walliams

Vain VALENTINE

Illustrated in
glorious colour by

Books

"Vain Valentine" from *The World's Worst Children 3*,
first published in Great Britain by
HarperCollins *Children's Books* in 2018

HarperCollins *Children's Books* is a division of HarperCollins*Publishers* Ltd,
HarperCollins Publishers
1 London Bridge Street
London SE1 9GF

The HarperCollins website address is
www.harpercollins.co.uk

Made for McDonald's in 2019

1

978-0-00-797648-5

David Walliams and Tony Ross assert the moral right to be
identified as the author and illustrator of the work respectively.

The National Literacy Trust is a registered charity no. 1116260 and a
company limited by guarantee no. 5836486 registered in England and Wales
and a registered charity in Scotland no. SC042944. Registered address:
68 South Lambeth Road, London SW8 1RL.

National Literacy Trust logo and reading tips copyright
© National Literacy Trust, 2019
literacytrust.org.uk

Batch No. 19966-04

Find out more about HarperCollins and the environment at
www.harpercollins.co.uk/green

Printed in China
THH
C4V

Are you ready to meet

VAIN VALENTINE?

SEARCH AND FIND: What is the smartest pupil in the school called?

Answer on page 60

Watch out for giggle-galore activities at the back!

Vain
VALENTINE

VALENTINE WAS HANDSOME, and boy did he **know it!** He was so **vain** he couldn't walk past a mirror without checking his **reflection** in it. One time, some boys at his school came into the toilets and caught Valentine **kissing** himself in the mirror.

Valentine believed that because he was **handsome** he should be famous too. He had **no** talents of any kind but, like a lot of **FAMOUS** people, he wasn't going to let **that** hold him back. The boy annoyed everyone by acting as if he were **FAMOUS**, strutting around the school wearing **sunglasses**. He never took them off, even when it was **dark,** and spent **all day bumping** into things as he couldn't see **where** he was going.

BOOF! "Ouch!"

If a teacher handed him a detention slip, he would assume they were asking for his **autograph**, scribble on it and hand it back to them.

"Have that framed! Instant heirloom!"

Valentine would refuse to take part in sports in case a stray ball bashed into his perfect face.

"Sorry, guys! My *face* is my

fortune! If I looked like you, I would be **broke!**"

Once, he developed a big red **spot** on the end of his nose, and was so horrified he didn't come into school for a whole term.

"NOOOOOO!
I thought I was
FLAWLESS!

ABSOLUTELY **FLAWLESS!**"

Valentine didn't have time for friends. Instead he spent the whole of break-time and lunchtime taking SELFIES.

CLICK!

At last count, he had $895,731$ pictures of himself on his phone. During any downtime, he would scroll through these, admiring **himself**.

CLICK!

CLICK!

CLICK!

CLICK!

"That's a **great** shot of **me. Another** great shot of **me.** Wow, yet another great shot of **me.** Why didn't anyone tell me I am SOOOOOO *handsome?*"

CLICK!

CLICK!

Valentine would claim that Valentine's
Day was named after **him.** He would

send hundreds of Valentine's cards to **himself,** which he would open during lessons to try to impress everybody.

"Oh no, this is **embarrassing!** Yet another card professing undying *love* for little old me!"

The girls in his school would **never** send him a card. He might have been *good-looking*, but his personality made him **repulsive.** Valentine really was one of the world's **worst** children.

MEET ME IN THE
SCHOOL PLAYGROUND
ON FRIDAY AT 4PM
FOR THE WORLD'S
BIGGEST GAME
OF KISS CHASE.

PRETTY GIRLS O

One day, Valentine had what he thought was a brilliant idea. An idea he was sure would propel him to stardom, **SUPERSTARDOM** or even **MEGASTARDOM.** He would enter the record books by setting a new world record for the biggest game of *kiss chase* ever. Valentine

IRLS, THIS IS YOUR CHANCE F A LIFETIME TO KISS THE HANDSOMEST BOY IN THE SCHOOL, IF NOT THE WORLD: VALENTINE. (OF COURSE.)

MEET ME IN THE SCHOOL PLAYGROUND ON FRIDAY AT 4PM FOR THE WORLD'S BIGGEST GAME OF KISS CHASE.

PRETTY GIRLS ONLY, PLEASE.

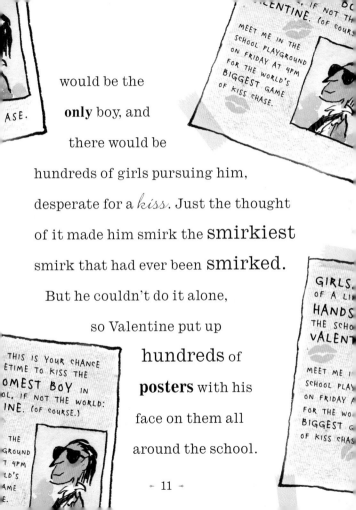

would be the

only boy, and

there would be

hundreds of girls pursuing him,

desperate for a *kiss*. Just the thought

of it made him smirk the smirkiest

smirk that had ever been smirked.

But he couldn't do it alone,

so Valentine put up

hundreds of

posters with his

face on them all

around the school.

What Valentine
didn't know was
that **none** of
the girls in his
school **wanted** to
kiss him.
In fact,
they found
his vanity
loathsome,

and he was a complete joke. The "PRETTY

GIRLS ONLY, PLEASE" part made them

loathe him even more.

The **smartest** pupil in the school was named Emmeline. As soon as she saw the posters go up, she spread word around the school that **all** the girls should meet in secret, as she had a **plan** that would teach this idiot boy a **lesson**.

The next morning, they all
gathered in the sports hall
before lessons began.
Emmeline climbed on to
a gym box so she could
address the crowd.

"Sisters!"

she began. Emmeline had a slight lisp, which only made her sound brainier than she already was. "I am sure you have all seen the **disgusting** posters *vain* Valentine has put up all over the school?"

There was a chorus of "Yes" followed by some loud **booing**.

"BOO!"

"How dare he write 'PRETTY GIRLS ONLY'?! Every single one of us, no matter what we look like, is beautiful."

There was a huge cheer from the crowd.

"HOORAY!"

"And we must teach this revolting creature a lesson!"

"YES!" went the crowd.

"But how?" asked a girl at the back, named Sylvia.

"He wants a *kiss chase*. So let's give him a *kiss chase*."

The girls looked at each other and began to murmur. How would that teach Valentine a lesson?

Emmeline smiled. She knew what was coming. "Let's chase him all the way **out** of this school!"

"YES!" The girls broke out into wild applause.

"With any luck, he might **never** come back!"

Emmeline expounded upon her **plan**, and swore all the girls to secrecy.

On Friday afternoon, just before four o'clock, Valentine made his way to the playground. There he met with the official from the world-records book.

She was a **stern-looking** woman, dressed in a blazer and skirt, holding a clipboard. Things got off to a *frosty* start.

"Hi, **babes!**" said Valentine, bounding up to her. He lifted his dark glasses. "Yes, it's really **me**. Valentine *Glorious*." Yes, that really **was** his surname.

"My name is Miss Pankhurst, Mr Glorious," replied the lady. "And I am certainly **not** your **'babe'**."

The boy was taken aback. In his head, **every** female on the planet adored him. "I said **'babes'** not **'babe'**."

"Well, that is not only patronising, but also grammatically **incorrect**. Now, **where** are all these girls for your world-record attempt? You can't do a *kiss chase* on your **own**!"

Valentine looked around the empty playground. "Don't worry, **babes**, I mean,

Miss Pankhurst. All the **chicks**..."

The lady gave the boy a **filthy** look.

Valentine continued to dig himself

deeper.

"I mean **honeys**, no... **dolls**... erm...

chicks?"

"Why don't you just call them

'ladies', Mr Glorious?"

"Ladies? I had never thought of that.

Yes, all right, then – MY ladies."

Miss Pankhurst shook her head as all

the young ladies in the school **marched**

on to the playground, led by Emmeline.

A smug smile spread across Valentine's

face. This was his **dream.** Not only were

hundreds of girls going

to chase him for a *kiss* but he would

enter the record books and become

A STAR.

Valentine studied the crowd,

and his smile turned to a

scowl. "I did say pretty girls

only!"

The girls all **tutted** their

disapproval. What a truly

despicable child he was.

Miss Pankhurst rolled her

eyes and took over. "Right,

ladies. If I could have you

all standing **behind** that white line,

please. Thank you so much. This is the

world-record attempt for the **largest-**

ever *kiss chase*. The current record

holder is pop star Mr Brad Bratters, who was chased by **three hundred and seventeen** of his fans after his concert in Las Vegas. They chased Mr Bratters all the way to the Grand Canyon, where he plummeted to his death. Which was a **sad** day for Mr

Bratters, if **not** for the people of the world, who will not miss Mr Bratters's smug little face and annoying songs. Still, it is, up to this point, the world's **largest** recorded *kiss chase*. I have counted **three hundred and forty-two** young ladies here today, comfortably clear of the current record.

Mr Glorious, are you **ready?"**

"I think I have a **hair** out of place!" said Valentine, stroking his fingers across his head.

All the girls
sighed and
ROLLED
their eyes. He
rushed to a
window and,
examining his
reflection, patted
the one tiny strand of hair that was **not**
slicked back perfectly with all the
others. Next, he took the opportunity
to smooth down his painstakingly
plucked eyebrows.

Finally, he winked at himself, and smiled before saying, "It's such a shame I can't **marry myself.**"

Emmeline mimed throwing up, which greatly amused the other girls.

"Ha! Ha!" they laughed.

" S H U S H ! " hissed Emmeline, not wanting Valentine to know they had a secret **plan.**

"Right. I am ready, **baby,**" announced the boy.

Miss Pankhurst grimaced.

"**Ladies**, are you ready?"

"**YES!**" they all chimed in together.
The girls of Valentine's school had been
waiting for this for a long, long time.

Behind their backs they were all
clasping **masks** they had made.

Every single one was of **Valentine.**

He had put so many posters of himself

up around the

school that it

was easy for

the girls to cut round his face and poke

through two eye holes.

Emmeline gave the order. **"Masks on, sisters!"**

It was a startling sight: 342 girls all looking **exactly** like the boy they were about to chase.

Valentine took in the scene. It was

FREAKY!

"W-w-what the...?" spluttered the boy.

But, before he could say whatever he was going to say next, Emmeline spoke up.

"You *love* **yourself** SO much, Valentine, that we thought you would like to be chased by your **own** stupid face!

Now,

CHARGE!"

Her **army of sisters** all started

running as if they were going into

BATTLE.

"NOOOOOOOOO!"

screamed Valentine, and he started

fleeing desperately across the

playground. **"HELP!"** he cried.

But **none** came.

Instead, **hundreds** of feet came pounding towards him. He passed a puddle. Valentine couldn't **resist** stopping to check his **reflection** in it. Even though his face was **STREAMING** with tears and snot,

Valentine
still
commented
on himself:

"Perfection!"

Unfortunately for Valentine, this stop to **admire** himself would prove to be his **undoing.** Together the girls of the school had the power of a herd of **STAMPEDING** wildebeest. Vain Valentine was trampled underfoot.

"STOP!" ordered Emmeline.

But it was too late.

The boy had been **FLATTENED** like a **pancake.**

The crowd parted. The girls took off their masks to look down at what they had done.

"Oh no," said Emmeline, full of sorrow. "I think we've **killed** him."

"Still, on the bright side, you have set a new **world record for the flattest boy ever,"** added Miss Pankhurst.

Silence descended upon the playground like thick **s n o w.**

"So I **am** going to be in the **world-record books!"** came a voice.

"I am going to be even more **FAMOUS**

than I already am, and I am already

very **FAMOUS**."

It was **Valentine.**

The **FLATTENED** boy rose slowly

to his feet.

He was now as tall and as wide

as a house.

"That is **great** news!"

"Yes... yes..."

replied Miss Pankhurst.

"I feel a bit **strange,**" said Valentine.

"Do I **look strange?**"

"No, no, no," muttered everyone unconvincingly.

Like a sail, he wafted over to a classroom window to take a look at the reflection of himself.

His face now resembled a dinner plate. In the centre was a **squashed** nose, and his eyes were now a skip away from each other. Valentine studied himself for a moment.

"Still **got it!**" he said.

All the girls looked on, open-mouthed in shock, as he billowed off.

"I hope for his sake there's not a gust of **wind**," remarked Emmeline, "or he might take off like a **kite.**"

"HA! HA! HA!"

they all laughed.

THE END

SELFIE SEARCH

Match up the selfie pairs.
Which selfie is the odd one out?

. . . .

CLICK!

CLICK!

CLICK!

CLICK!

CLICK!

ANSWER ON PAGE 60

AUTOGRAPH ARITHMETIC

Count how many autographs
Valentine has signed!

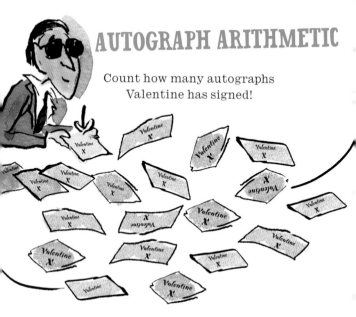

How many autographs did you find?

· · · · · · · · · · ·

Sign your autograph here!

ANSWER ON PAGE 60

I HEART ME!

Draw a picture of
yourself in the frame!

KITE COLOURING

Colour in the picture of Valentine floating away like a kite!

DOT-TO-DOT SQUASH

Join the dots to create
Valentine's squashed pancake face.
Don't forget to colour him in!

ANSWER ON PAGE 60

VALENTINE'S DAY QUIZ

Can you answer these questions about Valentine's story?

1 How long was Valentine out of school when he developed a big red spot on his nose?

A. A whole day

B. A whole term

C. A whole year

2 At his last count, how many pictures did Valentine have of himself on his phone?

A. 895

B. 89,573

C. 895,731

3 What does Valentine think he can set a new world record for?

A. Biggest game of kiss chase ever

B. Most autographs signed in an hour ever

C. Largest collection of selfies ever

ANSWERS ON PAGE 60

MIRROR MAZE

Vain Valentine needs to check his reflection.
Help him find the mirror as quickly as possible!

START

FINISH

ANSWER ON PAGE 60

MAKE YOUR OWN BOOK

Did you love this book? Why not make your own? Pick an adjective and character from the lists below to choose your title.

ADJECTIVES

1 Funny
2 Farting
3 Furious
4 Hairy
5 Happy
6 Hogging

PICK ONE

CHARACTERS

1 Footballer
2 Ferret
3 Fruit
4 Hamster
5 Hyena
6 Hairdresser

PICK ONE

My book title is

....

Using your title, design your
brilliant book cover here.

TITLE HERE

YOUR LOVELY
DRAWING HERE

AUTHOR NAME
HERE

ANSWERS

SEARCH-AND-FIND ANSWER: Emmeline on page 13

SELFIE SEARCH

1 and **8** **4** and **6**

2 and **9** **5** is the odd
one out

3 and **7**

AUTOGRAPH ARITHMETIC
20

DOT-TO-DOT SQUASH

VALENTINE'S DAY QUIZ

1 B. A whole term

2 C. 895,731

3 A. Biggest game of
kiss chase ever

MIRROR MAZE